The Golden .

عمر بن الخطاب رضي الله عنه – ثاني الخلفاء الراشدين

'Umar bin Al-Khattab رضي الله عنه

The Second Caliph of Islam

Second Edition: July 2004

© Maktaba Dar-us-Salam, 2000
King Fahd National Library Cataloging-in-Publication Data
Abdul Basit Ahmad
'Umar bin Al-Khattab: The Second Caliph of Islam-Riyadh.
48p., 14x21 cm. ISBN 9960-861-08-2
I-'Umar ibn Al-Khattab ibn Nufail II-Title
2- Prophet's Companions and Successors d. 23H
239.9 dc. 1923/16
Legal Deposit no. 1923/16
ISBN 9960-861-08-2

HEAD OFFICE

P.O. Box: 22743, Riyadh 11416 K.S.A.Tel: 00966-01-4033962/4043432 Fax: 4021659
E-mail: Riyadh@dar-us-salam.com, darussalam@awalnet.net.sa Website: www.dar-us-salam.com

K.S.A. Darussalam Showrooms:
Riyadh
Olaya branch: Tel 00966-1-4614483 Fax: 4644945
Malaz branch: Tel 4735220 Fax: 4735221
- **Jeddah**
  Tel: 00966-2-6879254 Fax: 6336270
- **Al-Khobar**
  Tel: 00966-3-8692900 Fax: 00966-3-8691551

U.A.E
- **Darussalam, Sharjah U.A.E**
  Tel: 00971-6-5632623 Fax: 5632624
  Sharjah@dar-us-salam.com

PAKISTAN
- **Darussalam,** 36 B Lower Mall, Lahore
  Tel: 0092-42-724 0024 Fax: 7354072
  Lahore@dar-us-salam.com
- Rahman Market, Ghazni Street
  Urdu Bazar Lahore
  Tel: 0092-42-7120054 Fax: 7320703

U.S.A
- **Darussalam, Houston**
  P.O Box: 79194 Tx 77279
  Tel: 001-713-722 0419 Fax: 001-713-722 0431
  E-mail: Webmaster@dar-us-salam.com
- **Darussalam, New York** 186 Atlantic Ave, Brooklyn
  New York-11217, Tel: 001-718-625 5925
  Fax: 718-625 1511
  Email: darussalamny@hotmail.com

U.K
- **Darussalam International Publications Ltd.**
  Leyton Business Centre
  Unit – 17, Etloe Road, Leyton, London, E10 7BT
  Tel: 00 44 20 8539 4885 Fax: 00 44 20 8539 4889
  Mobile: 00 44 7947 306 706
- **Darussalam International Publications Limited**
  146 Park Road,
  London NW8 7RG Tel: 00 44 20 725 2246
- **Darussalam**
  398-400 Coventry Road, Small Heath
  Birmingham, B10 0UF
  Tel: 0121 77204792 Fax: 0121 772 4345
  E-mail: info@darussalamuk.com
  Web: www.darussalamuk.com

FRANCE
- Editions & Librairie Essalam
  135, Bd de Ménilmontant- 75011 Paris
  Tél: 0033-01- 43 38 19 56/ 44 83
  Fax: 0033-01- 43 57 44 31
  E-mail: essalam@essalam.com

AUSTRALIA
- ICIS: Ground Floor 165-171, Haldon St.
  Lakemba NSW 2195, Australia
  Tel: 00612 9758 4040 Fax: 9758 4030

MALAYSIA
- E&D Books SDN. BHD.-321 B 3rd Floor,
  Suria Klcc
  Kuala Lumpur City Center 50088
  Tel: 00603-21663433
  Fax: 00603-42573758
  E-mail: endbook@tm.net.my

SINGAPORE
- Muslim Converts Association of Singapore
  32 Onan Road The Galaxy Singapore- 424484
  Tel: 0065-440 6924, 348 8344
  Fax: 440 6724

SRI LANKA
- Darul Kitab 6, Nimal Road, Colombo-4
  Tel: 0094-1-589 038 Fax: 0094-74 722433

KUWAIT
- Islam Presentation Committee
  Enlightment Book Shop
  P.O. Box: 1613, Safat 13017 Kuwait
  Tel: 00965-244 7526, Fax: 240 0057

INDIA
- Islamic Dimensions
  56/58 Tandel Street (North)
  Dongri, Mumbai 4000 009,India
  Tel: 0091-22-3736875, Fax: 3730689
  E-mail:sales@IRF.net

SOUTH AFRICA
- Islamic Da`wah Movement (IDM)
  48009 Qualbert 4078 Durban,South Africa
  Tel: 0027-31-304-6883
  Fax: 0027-31-305-1292
  E-mail: idm@ion.co.za

'Umar bin Al-Khattab رضي الله عنه
The Second Caliph of Islam

By
Abdul Basit Ahmad

Edited by
Aqeel Walker
Muhammad Ayub Sapra

DARUSSALAM
GLOBAL LEADER IN ISLAMIC BOOKS
Riyadh • Jeddah • Sharjah • Lahore
London • Houston • New York

بسم الله الرحمن الرحيم

In the Name of Allâh,
the Most Gracious, the Most Merciful

"Among the believers are men who have been true to their covenant with Allâh [i.e., they have gone out for *Jihâd* (holy fighting), and showed not their backs to the disbelievers]; of them some have fulfilled their obligations (i.e., have been martyred); and some of them are still waiting, but they have never changed (i.e., they never proved treacherous to their covenant which they concluded with Allâh) in the least." (33:23)

Publishers Note

All praises are due to Allâh, the Lord of all that exists. May Allâh's peace and blessings be upon His final Prophet and Messenger, Muhammad, his family and his Companions.

Darussalam is pleased to present this valuable series, '*The Golden Series of the Prophet's Companions*', to the Muslim youth. The purpose of these books is to enlighten our youth about the lives of the greatest heroes of Islam, the Prophet's Companions. Also, we wish to increase the enthusiasm of the Muslim youth for following and adhering to their religion. In this way, these books achieve two very important tasks: educating our youth and encouraging them to be good Muslims.

This book titled, '*Umar bin Al-Khattab* رضي الله عنه *– The Second Caliph of Islam*' is the life story of one of the closest Companions of the Prophet ﷺ. 'Umar رضي الله عنه was a bitter enemy of Islam but when he converted to Islam, Muslims felt strength enough to stand in any oppression. His life was a true dedication to the support of Islam and the Prophet ﷺ. When he emigrated to Al-Madinah in daylight. He challenged the chiefs of the Quraish to stop him but no one of them dared stand in his way. Although he was a senior Companion of the Prophet ﷺ but he convinced the *Ansâr* that Abu Bakr رضي الله عنه should be the first Caliph.

We hope that these books are beneficial to our Muslim youth, as they are the future of Islam. We, at Darussalam realize the importance of good Islamic literature for Muslim youth, especially in the West where non-Islamic influences are so strong. For this reason, we feel that the availability of this series will be a valuable aid in instilling a genuine love for Islam in our youth. We would like to thank the author, Mr. Abdul Basit Ahmad, the editors, Mr. Aqeel Walker and Mr. Muhammad Ayub Sapra for their diligent work in preparing this series. As Allâh says:

> "Is there any reward for good other than good?" (55:60)

And our final invocation is that all praises are due to Allâh, the Lord of all that exists.

Abdul Malik Mujahid
General Manager

Foreword

Human beings tend to be unjust in their dealings with each other, especially when there is no divine guidance that directs them to be just to each other. To act justly with others under all conditions, one must be endowed with the great blessings of self-denial and humility. Injustice becomes quite clear when it comes from a ruler, because abuse of power usually prevails in his dealings with his subjects unless he is guided by divine teachings.

Over history, few rulers have been rightfully called just. The most distinguished among those rulers is our hero, 'Umar bin Al-Khattab رضي الله عنه, the second Caliph of Islam.

'Umar رضي الله عنه excelled all examples of justice known before and after him except for the Prophet ﷺ, for he was the one who taught him how to be just toward others. He acted justly with all his subjects whether they were Muslims or non-Muslims. Not only this, but he also kept close control of the rulers whom he appointed in various parts of the Islamic State to ensure that they treated people with justice.

"In addition, 'Umar رضي الله عنه was so firm in his practice of Islam that he usually could sense what was right or wrong before the Prophet ﷺ had informed others of it. The Prophet ﷺ said about him:

> "Among the Children of Israel who lived before you, there were men who used to be inspired with guidance though they were not Prophets, and if there were any such person amongst my followers, it would be 'Umar."

To the story of this great man and ruler let us give an ear and from his honorable life let us learn a lesson.

Abdul Basit Ahmad

Introduction

The Prophet's Companions

"The Golden Series of the Prophet's Companions" was meant to instill the values and morals that the early Muslims adopted in their lives in the hearts of our youngsters in order that they may find their way through our present materialistic world.

The Prophet's Companion is defined as a person who believed in the Prophet ﷺ and came in contact with him. The Prophet ﷺ told about the future generations of believers and called them his "brothers". The Companions of the Prophet ﷺ exclaimed:

"Are not we your brothers?"

The Prophet ﷺ told them:

"You are my Companions. My brothers are those who would believe in me although they did not see me."

Seniority of the Prophet's Companions depended on their initiative to accept Islam, emigration to Al-Madinah and participation in the battle of Badr. Allâh confirmed this classification by placing the early Muslims of emigrants and supporters at the head of the list of believers.

The Prophet ﷺ said:

"The best people are those who live at my time (meaning his Companions), followed by those who come after them and the ones who come after the latter."

Therefore, we hold all of the Prophet's Companions to be good and we do not prefer some while hating others.

Some of the Prophet's Companions were foretold by the Prophet ﷺ that they would dwell in Paradise in the Hereafter. Also, the four rightly guided Caliphs of Islam are placed first on the list of the Companions of the Prophet ﷺ as they combined many characteristics that no other Companions had.

Some people of our time ignorantly criticize the Companions of the Prophet ﷺ. The Prophet ﷺ said:

"Do not say anything bad about my Companions…."

Therefore, we should respect all Companions of the Prophet ﷺ. We should also believe that they were the best men created by Allâh after the Prophets. They led a life of piety and devotion and followed the steps of the Prophet ﷺ. They were the living models of the teachings of the Qur'ân. They lived during the period that the Qur'ân was being revealed to the Prophet ﷺ and applied it in letter and spirit to their lives. They sacrificed all their resources to support the Word of Allâh. Whenever you read about them, you discover something new about their dedication and truthfulness.

These were the Companions of the Prophet ﷺ to whom we are greatly indebted, for had it not been for their sacrifices and devotion, we would not be Muslims today.

Background

'Umar bin Al-Khattab belonged to a clan of high rank amongst the Quraish tribe. He was born forty years before the emigration of the Muslims to Al-Madinah in a house of dignity and honour. His father, Al-

Khattab, was the chief of the Bani Makhzoum clan.

When 'Umar was a boy, his father treated him very harshly. He usually spent most of his time in the desert grazing camels for his father. However, when he became a young man, he began learning how to be a good merchant. He was also trained in wrestling and horsemanship until he became an example of strength and skill in both arts.

At that time, the Arabs were mostly illiterate. A few people knew how to read and write Arabic. 'Umar began learning how to read and write Arabic, which he mastered within a short period.

While still young, 'Umar traveled to many countries as a merchant and met many prominent people in both Syria and Iraq. He also acquired good knowledge of the affairs of the Roman and Persian Empires which were governing the world at that time.

'Umar was a well-known personality all over the Arabian Peninsula. He was also feared by other chiefs because of his strength and position amongst the Quraish tribe.

When Muhammad ﷺ proclaimed the message of Islam, ‘Umar took the side of the opposition. He was very hard on the few early Muslims. He used to beat his housemaid harshly because she accepted Islam. He did his best to make her and the other new Muslims abandon their faith. His relatives who accepted Islam kept their conversion to Islam secret for fear that he might torture them.

Intentions to kill the Prophet ﷺ

'Umar knew how steadfast the Muslims were to their faith. He used all means to make them go back to the worship of idols, but his efforts were all in vain. Therefore, he decided to kill the Prophet ﷺ himself in order to put an end to the message of Islam.

In a moment of rage, 'Umar took his sword and headed to the place where the Prophet ﷺ was teaching his followers the principles of Islam. On the way there, he met one of his tribesmen named Na'eem bin 'Abdullah , who had already accepted Islam but kept it secret. Na'eem saw the signs of anger on 'Umar's face. He asked him where he was going. 'Umar angrily replied that he was going to kill Muhammad because he abused the idols of the Arabs. Na'eem wanted 'Umar to change his direction. Therefore, he told him that it was better for him to settle his case with his sister and her husband before killing Muhammad ﷺ.

'Umar was astonished to learn that his

sister, Fatimah, and her husband, Sa'eed, had accepted Islam. He changed his way and hurried to his sister's house. Upon arriving there, he stood at the door listening. To his surprise, he heard his sister, her husband and a third person reading the Qur'ân. He knocked at the door and waited for someone to open it. His sister immediately hid the papers they were reading and asked Khabbâb bin Al-Aratt رضي الله عنه, the teacher, to hide. She opened the door and came face to face with 'Umar. He immediately asked her what they were reading. She denied reading anything. He slapped her on the face. Her nose began bleeding. Her husband tried to interfere but 'Umar pushed him back harshly. Fatimah decided that it was better to tell him the truth. She strongly said that she and her husband had accepted Islam and that they would not change their faith even if he killed them.

Signs of the Change

'Umar looked at his sister's face with her bleeding nose. His anger vanished and he felt sorry for what he had done. He calmly asked her to show him what they were reading. She gave him the papers and 'Umar began reading the Verses of the Qur'ân:

"*Tâ-Hâ*. We have not sent down the Qur'ân to you (O Muhammad ﷺ) to cause distress. But only as a Reminder to those who fear (Allâh). A revelation from Him (Allâh) Who created the earth and high heavens." (20:1-4)

'Umar's face began changing and his heart softened. He felt a serenity that he had never felt before. Tears began rolling down his cheeks as a result of the impact of the nice words he was reading. He immediately asked his sister's husband to take him to the Prophet ﷺ. Upon hearing these words, Khabbab bin Al-Aratt رضي الله عنه left his hiding place and told 'Umar that he had heard the Prophet ﷺ praying to Allâh to guide 'Umar to the way of Islam. He told 'Umar that the Prophet ﷺ and his Companions were in Dar Al-Arqam house.

Meeting the Prophet ﷺ

'Umar apologized for his rudeness toward his sister and her husband and left to the place where the Prophet ﷺ and his Companions gathered. He knocked at the door and waited for someone to open. A Companion of the Prophet ﷺ peeped through the cracks of the door and saw 'Umar with a sword at his side standing at the door. He told the Prophet ﷺ that it was 'Umar. the Companions of the Prophet ﷺ felt afraid because they knew how hard 'Umar was on the Muslims. The Prophet ﷺ asked the man to open the door. As 'Umar went in, the Prophet ﷺ threatened him that he feared that Allâh would punish him for his cruelty towards the Muslims. He then asked him about the reason for coming to him. 'Umar immediately said that he came to embrace Islam. The Muslims inside the room were very happy to hear these words from 'Umar.

'Umar declares His Conversion to Islam Publicly

Immediately after embracing Islam, 'Umar رضي الله عنه went to the Ka'bah and announced before the chiefs of the Quraish that he had believed in Islam and the Prophet ﷺ and that he would challenge them till the end of his life. A fight ensued and the pagans attacked 'Umar رضي الله عنه, but he bravely fought them all until an elderly man came and convinced the people to leave 'Umar رضي الله عنه alone. From that day on, the Muslims felt strong and began worshipping Allâh openly. Historians confirmed that 'Umar رضي الله عنه embraced Islam six years after the Prophet ﷺ was commissioned to proclaim the message of Islam. 'Abdullah bin Mas'ûd رضي الله عنه said:

> "After 'Umar accepted Islam we gained power and respect."

Oppression and Tyranny

The Muslims received all types of persecution at the hands of the chiefs of the Quraish. Many of them migrated to Abyssinia to escape the torture that the Quraish inflicted on them. 'Umar ﷺ and his fellow Muslims were striving to keep steadfast to their faith. Weak people and slaves who believed in the message of Islam were not able to withstand the oppression of the Quraish.

Attempts to Seek Protection

The Prophet ﷺ felt that there was no way out of such oppression but to emigrate to another land. He began calling tribes outside of Makkah to accept Islam and provide protection to him and his Companions. However, the chiefs of the Quraish were following his steps and defaming him before the visitors of Makkah.

The Prophet ﷺ decided to visit Tâ'if, a city near Makkah, to seek protection, but the chiefs of the Thaqeef tribe treated him very badly and rejected his call.

A group of people from a city called Yathrib (later known as Al-Madinah) visited Makkah. The Prophet ﷺ called them to accept Islam and provide protection for the Muslims. The group of people accepted the call and promised to come the next year with their chiefs to make an agreement with the Prophet ﷺ.

Islam spread quickly in Al-Madinah. Seventy men and a few women visited Makkah that year to hold a pledge of loyalty with the Prophet ﷺ. They promised to provide all means possible to protect the Prophet ﷺ and his followers in their city. It should be noted that emigration was an act ordained by Allâh through the Prophet ﷺ and not only an act to have protection against persecution and oppression of the Quraish.

'Umar رضي الله عنه emigrates to Al-Madinah

'Umar and twenty people of his clan emigrated to Al-Madinah in daylight. He challenged the chiefs of the Quraish to stop him but no one of them dared stand in his way.

Upon arriving in Al-Madinah, 'Umar رضي الله عنه settled at a place called Quba' near Al-Madinah. He and his fellow Muslims received a warm welcome in Al-Madinah. The Prophet ﷺ and his close Companion Abu Bakr رضي الله عنه followed them after a short time. The first thing the Prophet ﷺ did after settling in Al-Madinah was strengthening the ties of Islamic brotherhood between the emigrants (from

Makkah) and supporters (inhabitants of Al-Madinah). 'Umar ﵁ was made the brother in Islam of 'Utban bin Malik ﵁, the chief of Bani Saleem clan. 'Umar ﵁ joined his brothers in Islam in establishing firm foundations for the new state. He also joined hands with the other Muslims in building the first mosque of Islam. The Prophet ﷺ discussed with his Companions a way to call the Muslims to prayer. Some of them suggested ringing a bell at times of prayer, some suggested blowing a horn and others proposed to raise a flag. The Prophet ﷺ did not support any of these suggestions. He wanted to have something special for the Muslims.

'Umar ﵁ was very concerned about finding a way to call to prayer. That very night he had a dream. A man holding a bell came to him. 'Umar ﵁ asked him to give him the bell to use it to call the Muslims to prayer. However, the man told him that he had something better than the bell. He told him that it was better to call to prayer by using the *Adhân*. The next morning, 'Umar ﵁ hurried to the Prophet ﷺ to tell him about the dream he had. Surprisingly, another man had the same dream. He told the Prophet ﷺ about his dream before 'Umar ﵁ did. The Prophet ﷺ welcomed the idea and asked Bilal ﵁ to climb on top of the roof of the mosque to call the Muslims to prayer.

Challenges to Islam

Attempts to recover the Stolen Property

When 'Umar رضي الله عنه and his fellow Muslims emigrated to Al-Madinah, they left behind all their property in Makkah, which the pagans took. The Muslims wanted to recover their property. A caravan led by Abu Sufyan was heading to Makkah back from Damascus loaded with all types of goods. The Prophet ﷺ instructed his Companions to capture the caravan. However, Abu Sufyan knew of the plan and changed his way. At the same time, he sent a man to the Quraish to warn them.

The Battle of Badr

The pagans gathered an army of about one thousand fighters and headed to Al-Madinah to save their caravan and to put an end to the threats of the Muslims. Although they were informed that the caravan had escaped from the Muslims, they insisted on fighting the Muslims and destroying their new state.

The Prophet ﷺ and his Companions received news of this huge army. They discussed how to face the challenge. They barely gathered an army of three hundred and thirteen fighters and marched to a place called Badr near Al-Madinah. 'Umar رضي الله عنه prepared himself for the first battle against those who treated the Muslims with cruelty. He decided to show them that although the Muslims were weak, they could defeat the idolaters with the support of Allâh and strong Faith.

The battle started fiercely. 'Umar's main concern was to protect his Faith. During the battle, he came face to face with his uncle. He did not hesitate to kill his uncle because the latter came with the intention to destroy Islam. Although the number of the Muslim army was small compared to the number of their enemy, they defeated them. Seventy of the pagans were killed in the battle and the Muslims took another seventy soldiers as prisoners of war.

Revelation Supports 'Umar's Point of View

Upon returning to Al-Madinah, the Prophet ﷺ discussed with his Companions the issue of the prisoners of war. Abu Bakr رضي الله عنه convinced the Prophet ﷺ that it would be better to take ransom money from them while 'Umar رضي الله عنه insisted on killing them because they were the aggressors. However, the Prophet ﷺ took the side of Abu Bakr رضي الله عنه. A while later, revelation came down supporting 'Umar's point of view that the prisoners of war should have been killed so that they could not fight against the Muslims again.

Other Challenges Against Islam

'Umar ﷺ continued his struggle for the sake of Islam. He did not miss any chance that would add to the strength of the newborn state of Islam. In the battle of Uhud, he and the other Muslims fought a hard battle. Although the Muslims lost the battle, 'Umar ﷺ and his fellow Muslims kept steadfast to their faith. Two years later, the pagans gathered a huge army and wanted to destroy the Islamic State. However, 'Umar ﷺ and the other Muslims dug a trench around Al-Madinah that stopped the pagans and prevented them from entering the city. After a siege for one month, the pagans withdrew in humiliation back to Makkah.

The Treaty

One year later, the Prophet ﷺ and his Companions wanted to visit Makkah to perform '*Umrah*. Although the Muslims wanted their journey to be peaceful, the pagans prevented them from entering Makkah. At a place called Al-Hudaibiyah, the Prophet ﷺ and his Companions negotiated with the Makkans to reach a peace agreement. The pagans insisted on putting a condition in the agreement stating that if anyone from the Muslims wished to join the pagans he should be given the freedom to do so, but if anyone from the pagans wished to join the Muslims, he should be sent back to the pagans by the Muslims. 'Umar رضي الله عنه felt that this condition was humiliating to the Muslims. He was very angry and wanted the Prophet ﷺ to refuse such an unjust condition. The Prophet ﷺ told him that he was the Messenger of Allâh and that Allâh would support him. Later on, 'Umar رضي الله عنه knew that the agreement was in the good interest of the Muslims. It gave the Muslims a chance to stop fighting with the main power in the Arabian Peninsula and call other tribes of Arabia to Islam. Several tribes accepted Islam and joined in building the Islamic State.

Conquest of Makkah

The Quraish failed to respect their agreement with the Muslims. They broke their promise and killed some of the Muslims' allies. The Prophet ﷺ and the Muslims were now determined to put an end to idolatry in Makkah. 'Umar رضي الله عنه joined the army of ten thousand Muslims who marched to Makkah and conquered the city. 'Umar رضي الله عنه wanted to revenge himself against the pagans who oppressed the Muslims. However, the Prophet ﷺ taught him that a triumphant believer should always be forgiving. The

Prophet ﷺ told the people of Makkah that they were free. In reaction to this merciful attitude by the Prophet ﷺ, all the people of Makkah accepted Islam. 'Umar رضي الله عنه was beside the Prophet ﷺ when the women of Makkah came to embrace Islam. The Prophet ﷺ asked 'Umar رضي الله عنه to be his deputy in witnessing the acceptance of Islam by the women.

The Prophet Passes Away

As Makkah had now become a Muslim land, the Prophet ﷺ told his Companions that he wished to perform pilgrimage. 'Umar رضي الله عنه, along with one hundred thousand Muslims, accompanied the Prophet ﷺ to Makkah to perform pilgrimage. Upon completing the pilgrimage rites, the Prophet ﷺ addressed his Companions about the everlasting principles of Islam. In his speech, he implied that he would pass away soon. 'Umar رضي الله عنه felt very sad to hear these words from the Prophet ﷺ. Upon returning to Al-Madinah, the Prophet ﷺ fell ill. After a short period, he passed away. When 'Umar رضي الله عنه was told that the Prophet ﷺ had passed away, he did not believe the news. He unsheathed his sword and threatened to kill anyone who might say that the Prophet ﷺ had died. He loved the Prophet ﷺ dearly and wanted him to remain alive among the Muslims to direct them if they did something wrong. He was calmed down and convinced by Abu Bakr رضي الله عنه that the Prophet ﷺ had died indeed.

The Selection of the Caliph

While 'Umar رضي الله عنه and other close Companions of the Prophet ﷺ were busy with the Prophet's funeral, a group from the *Ansâr* (supporters) gathered at a place called As-Saqifah to select a caliph (ruler) from among them. Someone told 'Umar رضي الله عنه of this meeting and he along with Abu Bakr رضي الله عنه and Abu 'Ubaidah bin Al-Jarrah رضي الله عنه left the funeral and went to As-Saqifah. 'Umar رضي الله عنه convinced the supporters that Abu Bakr رضي الله عنه should be the Caliph. They all accepted his selection of Abu Bakr رضي الله عنه and pledged obedience.

‘Umar رضي الله عنه, the Caliph

Before passing away, Abu Bakr رضي الله عنه consulted the senior Companions of the Prophet ﷺ about the best man to succeed him. They all agreed that ‘Umar رضي الله عنه would be the best Caliph.

As ‘Umar رضي الله عنه took over, he started organizing the affairs of the state relying on the teachings of the Qur’ân and the Prophet’s sayings.

Achievements of ‘Umar رضي الله عنه during His Rule

With the spread of the Islamic State over Iraq, Syria and Egypt, ‘Umar رضي الله عنه found it necessary to establish firm regulations under which the rulers of different regions should deal with their subjects. He sent letters containing rules of government to the governors. Not only this, but he also made visits to some parts of the Islamic Empire to ensure that the governors he appointed were treating people justly.

‘Umar رضي الله عنه also established the public treasury. The money brought to the treasury was equally distributed among the Muslims. Records of soldiers were made so as to pay them their wages wherever they were. The army was organized in a way very similar to the modern armies. Every seven soldiers were headed by a supervisor who was responsible for their wages and benefits. ‘Umar رضي الله عنه also appointed judges to solve problems among the Muslims. He himself was summoned before the judge on at least two occasions. He recruited watchmen to guard the streets during the night and established a system of controls on markets to prevent any ways of deceit.

Public facilities and construction of cities were also part of his interests. He ordered the building of Kufah, Basrah and Mausil in Iraq and Fustat and Jiza in Egypt . He himself prepared the layouts of these cities. Spaces for streets and alleys were determined by ‘Umar رضي الله عنه himself. Rivers and canals were also dug to provide water to populated areas all over the Islamic State. Engineers and craftsmen from all parts of the state were mobilized to pave roads in order for caravans to travel with ease throughout the vast state.

'Umar ﵁ found that it was essential for all Muslims to learn how to read the Qur'ân. Therefore, he sent teachers to all parts of the state to teach people how to recite the Noble Qur'ân. He also set prizes for those who memorized the Qur'ân within a short period. Scholars among the Prophet's Companions were directed to teach people the interpretation of the Qur'ân and the principles of the *Sharî'ah* (Islamic law). Bedouins were given much attention. Teaching of their children was established as a mandatory law. *Muftis* (legal advisors) were also appointed to give answers to legal questions.

'Umar ﵁ paid much attention to construction of mosques. He gave orders to expand the Sacred Mosque in Makkah as its space was not sufficient to accommodate visitors. He also supervised expansion of the

Prophet's Mosque in Al-Madinah for the same reasons. He wrote to all governors ordering them to build mosques in cities and villages. It is reported that the number of mosques built during 'Umar's rule was more than three thousand.

The Arabs had no certain event to set the calendar. 'Umar رضي الله عنه was receiving letters from governors that were not dated with a year. He discussed the matter with his advisors. They all agreed to his point of view that the year of the *Hijrah* (emigration to Al-Madinah) should be the first year of the Islamic calendar.

As most people of the conquered lands, especially Iraq, Syria and Egypt were farmers, 'Umar رضي الله عنه ordered for their lands to be kept under their own control because they were familiar with the methods of cultivation. In addition, he provided farmers with all means necessary to increase and diversify their crops.

In addition to the records and

bureaus, 'Umar, رضي الله عنه established for the military and civilians of the Islamic society, he ordered construction of barracks for the army at the borders of the Islamic State. This allowed the soldiers to use these as places of residence away from their homeland. He also set rules of service for soldiers. No soldier should keep away from his family more than four months so as to keep in touch with his family. Mail from soldiers was sometimes distributed by 'Umar رضي الله عنه himself.

As the road from Al-Madinah to Makkah was hard for pilgrims and visitors, 'Umar رضي الله عنه gave orders to pave the road, establish shaded rest places and dig wells to provide water to caravans.

Care for the Nation

The services rendered during the rule of 'Umar رضي الله عنه did not cover Muslims only but were extended to all the subjects of the state. Old non-Muslim men and women were given maintenance pay. Subsidies were also given to farmers and craftsmen to help them continue their businesses. Every poor member of the nation was receiving a welfare stipend including newborns.

Honorable Treatment of Conquered People

Palestine was mainly inhabited by Christians. When the Muslims conquered it, the inhabitants of *Al-Quds* (Jerusalem) agreed to surrender the city peacefully to the Muslim army. They knew that 'Umar رضي الله عنه was a just ruler. Therefore, they wanted him to sign the agreement himself. 'Umar رضي الله عنه left Al-Madinah and visited *Al-Quds* to make the agreement. It was reported that he was not accompanied by any guards except his servant. He concluded an agreement with the inhabitants of the city, which guaranteed them all their financial and religious rights. As a result, most of the city inhabitants accepted Islam.

Conquests under 'Umar's Rule

Conquests in Iraq and Iran

During Abu Bakr's rule, the Muslim armies spread east and north for the propagation of Islam. Before conquering the Persians and the Romans, Abu Bakr رضي الله عنه died and left the trust to 'Umar رضي الله عنه. 'Umar رضي الله عنه continued the efforts started by Abu Bakr رضي الله عنه to conquer the two major nations of the time.

'Umar رضي الله عنه selected Sa'd bin Abi Waqqâs رضي الله عنه to conquer Persia. An army of thirty thousand soldiers was gathered to fulfil the mission. Before leaving Al-Madinah, 'Umar رضي الله عنه advised Sa'd رضي الله عنه saying:

"Sa'd, I order you to fight the Persians. Listen to me and hold fast to my words. You are going to face a very hard obstacle that you cannot overcome unless you observe truth and goodness. You should know that every battle should be prepared for by having good equipment. Let your equipment be patience. Do not be deceived by saying to yourself 'I am the Prophet's uncle' for there is no kinship dearer to Allâh than obedience to His teachings."

Sa'd رضي الله عنه led the army to a place called Al-Qâdisiyah in Iraq. There he saw the Persians deploying their army under the leadership of Rustam.

'Umar رضي الله عنه wrote a letter to Sa'd رضي الله عنه saying:

"I order you and your soldiers to fear Allâh at all times, for fearing Allâh is the best weapon you have against your enemy. I order you and your soldiers to guard against evil deeds as much as you guard against your enemy. Evil deeds are more dangerous to your army than your enemy is. You will win because your enemy is a disbeliever. Ask Allâh to help you overcome your desires as much as you ask Him to help you overcome your enemy. Do not cause Muslims to march when they are tired and keep them ready with full strength to meet the enemy. Take rest one day every week to keep your army fully ready. Do not come near any village inhabited by our protected peaceful allies and do not allow anyone of your army to enter any village unless you are sure he will act properly. Lookout scouting is the best way to know the power of your enemy. Therefore, give such a mission to whom you most trust and provide them with the best horses."

Sa‘d رضي الله عنه sent messengers to Yazdajurd, the Persian King, calling him to embrace Islam, to pay tribute or if he rejected both options, to fight.

The first delegation called the King to accept Islam. Instead of accepting this kind call, the King began blaming the Muslims for coming to his land and threatened to destroy their religion. The King showed the delegation much humiliation and anger. He asked his soldiers to fill sacks of soil and force the members of the delegation to carry them on their backs till they left the city. He told them that he would send Rustam to bury their leader and the Muslim army in Al-Qâdisiyah trench.

Rustam foresaw signs of defeat in the acts of the King. Therefore, he asked Sa‘d رضي الله عنه to send him another messenger to negotiate.

Al-Mugheerah bin Shu'bah رضي الله عنه came to Rustam. As soon as he arrived, Rustam started negotiating with him in a very gentle manner and asked him to tell Sa'd رضي الله عنه that it was better for the Muslims to leave to their homeland. Al-Mugheerah رضي الله عنه told Rustam that it was their mission to spread the light of Islam. He explained to him the principles of Islam.

Rustam felt the just teachings of Islam and asked the messenger to give him time to discuss them with the heads of the nation. Rustam told his people that it was better for them to accept Islam, but they refused.

Sa'd رضي الله عنه sent the third messenger, Reb'iy bin 'Amir رضي الله عنه to Rustam. Before his arrival to the place of the Persian army, the Persians wanted to show him how rich and powerful they were. The whole palace was furnished with gold and silver. Reb'iy رضي الله عنه came inside with his humble dress on his horse until he stepped on the carpets and spoilt them with his spear. He jumped down from the back of his horse and sat beside Rustam. He was not amazed by the vanity they wanted to show him. The negotiations did not yield any fruits.

More messengers were sent but all

attempts to reach a solution came to nothing. At last, Rustam told Sa'd رضي الله عنه that he would give the Muslims a bitter defeat if they insisted on fighting.

The Persians prepared about one hundred thousand fully armed soldiers supported by elephants and other heavy combat equipment. The Muslims on the opposite side gathered their humble arms to fight against this huge army.

The timing of operations was initiated by the words *Allâhu Akbar* (Allâh is the Greatest). The Muslim army faced a sudden shock. Their horses did not move forward for fear of the advancing elephants that the Persians put in the first line. However, some Muslim fighters began shooting the elephants. They forced the elephants to retreat in terror and throw off their riders. The whole day of fighting did not change the positions of either army. The second day a new round of fighting started. The Muslims received support by an army led by Hashim bin 'Utbah رضي الله عنه coming from Damascus. However, victory was achieved by neither army.

On the third day, the Persians

prepared for another surprise. They put some huge elephants ahead of the army and attacked the Muslim army. The attack was almost successful. However, some Muslim commandos led by Al-Qa‘qâ‘ bin ‘Amr رضي الله عنه attacked the elephants and forced them to turn back through the advancing army. The Muslims then opened huge gaps through the Persian army.

The battle continued and the Muslims were sacrificing their souls to raise the Islamic banner high. The fighting went on all the night. When the sun rose, it was clear that the Muslims had the upper hand.

Rustam tried to escape but he was finally killed. The succeeding commander, Galinos, tried to save the defeated army by crossing to the other bank of the Tigris River. Instead, more than thirty thousand of his soldiers drowned in the river.

Sa‘d رضي الله عنه ordered his army to follow the fleeing army until he was sure that victory was fully achieved. The battle was over and Sa‘d رضي الله عنه immediately sent a messenger to ‘Umar رضي الله عنه informing him of the victory they achieved and asking for further orders. 'Umar رضي الله عنه ordered Sa'd رضي الله عنه to continue his march to Mada'in, the Persian capital. The Muslims marched forth but did not meet any resistance on the way to the capital.

The Muslim army led by Sa'd رضي الله عنه did not have any boats to cross the Tigris River. Sa'd رضي الله عنه ordered his soldiers to cross the river on horse backs. Not one of them was stopped by the torrent of the river. The Persian soldiers on the opposite bank of the river thought that they were fighting against genies. Salman Al-Farisi رضي الله عنه (a great Companion of the Prophet, ﷺ originally from Persia) foresaw the heavenly help given to Muslims. He shouted:

> "I swear by Allâh, those who had overcome the mainland would surely overcome the sea."

The Muslim army surprised the Persian army who fled the city. Mada'in was conquered and the Persian Empire was defeated forever.

Conquests in Syria and Palestine

Abu Bakr رضي الله عنه appointed Khalid bin Al-Waleed رضي الله عنه as Commander General of the Muslim army. He was fighting the Persians in Iraq but was directed by Abu Bakr رضي الله عنه to support the army led by Abu 'Ubaidah bin Al-Jarrah رضي الله عنه who was directed to conquer the Romans.

The Romans gathered an army of two hundred thousand soldiers while the Muslim army numbered about thirty thousand fighters. Both armies met near a village called Al-Yarmouk. Khalid رضي الله عنه carefully studied the conditions and set up plans to fight the coming battle.

Before the start of the battle, the Roman commander sought to meet Khalid رضي الله عنه. He agreed to meet with him. The Roman commander addressed Khalid رضي الله عنه saying:

> "It has been brought to our knowledge that poverty was the only reason that brought you out of your land to here. If you wish, I will give each one of you ten dinars, clothes and food on the condition that you go back to your land. I will even reward you with equal portions next year."

Khalid رضي الله عنه angrily responded to such a

belittling address saying:

> "It is not poverty that brought us here; rather, it is that we only wish to drink your blood. We have been told it is most tasty."

Khalid ﷺ returned to his troops. He studied the battlefield and decided to divide his army into battalions along the line of combat to face the huge number of the Roman army.

Soon the rattle of swords and cries of *Allâhu Akbar* (Allâh is the Greatest) filled the air and heads fell under horses' hooves. Both armies fought all day long. They became very tired and retreated to their original positions. On the next day, Khalid ﷺ and his soldiers attacked the heart of the Roman army and divided their lines. The Romans, on the other side, began retreating and fleeing in all directions. They suffered a huge loss and left the battlefield in humiliation.

While the battle was hot, a messenger from Al-Madinah arrived with news that Abu Bakr ﷺ had died, that 'Umar ﷺ was selected as the Caliph and that Khalid ﷺ was to be replaced by Abu

'Ubaidah bin Al-Jarrah رضي الله عنه. Abu 'Ubaidah رضي الله عنه kept the news secret until the Romans were finally defeated. He met Khalid رضي الله عنه and informed him of the news. Khalid رضي الله عنه willingly handed over the command to Abu 'Umbaidah رضي الله عنه and continued as an ordinary soldier under Abu 'Ubaidah's command. Abu 'Ubaidah رضي الله عنه continued his march. He conquered Damascus and its surrounding areas. The Roman Emperor left his place of rule in Hims and paid Syria an eternal farewell. Following this great victory, Abu 'Ubaidah رضي الله عنه led his army to *Al-Quds* (Jerusalem). The chiefs of the city surrendered the city peacefully. They asked the leader to make an agreement which, upon their request, was to be signed by 'Umar رضي الله عنه himself.

Conquest of Egypt

'Umar رضي الله عنه continued his efforts of spreading the light of Islam. He prepared an army under the leadership of 'Amr bin Al-'Aas رضي الله عنه to conquer Egypt. Within a short period of time, 'Amr رضي الله عنه defeated the Romans and saved the Egyptians from their injustices. He built a strong Muslim state in Egypt under the guidance of 'Umar bin Al-Khattab رضي الله عنه.

Humility

‘Umar رضي الله عنه was known as a very humble man. He used to help the orphans and widows to manage their lives. Once he was walking with his servant through the streets of Al-Madinah during the night. He heard some children crying. He found that a poor woman was trying to calm down her hungry children by putting an empty pot on the fire to show them that she was making them some food. ‘Umar رضي الله عنه went back to the warehouse and took some flour and meat, carried them on his back and returned to the woman. He began cooking for the children and giving them food. He left them very happy. It was reported that he also visited an old woman every night to care for her and satisfy her needs.

Justice

A Jew complained against ‘Umar to the judge, ‘Ali bin Abi Talib رضي الله عنه. ‘Ali رضي الله عنه summoned ‘Umar رضي الله عنه and the Jew before him to settle the case. ‘Umar رضي الله عنه was very happy that ‘Ali رضي الله عنه made him stand beside the Jew in the court and did not distinguish him over the Jew.

The son of 'Amr bin Al-'Aas رضي الله عنه, the governor of Egypt, entered a race on horses with an Egyptian. The Egyptian won the race. 'Amr's son got angry and whipped the Egyptian because he won the race. The Egyptian came to 'Umar complaining against 'Amr's son. 'Umar رضي الله عنه sent for 'Amr رضي الله عنه and his son to appear before him. Upon appearing before him, 'Umar رضي الله عنه asked the Egyptian to whip 'Amr's son as he had whipped him. 'Umar رضي الله عنه addressed 'Amr رضي الله عنه saying:

> "Since when do you started to enslave people when they were born free."

Fear of Allâh

'Umar رضي الله عنه was always expressing his fear of meeting Allâh on the Day of Judgment with any sins. Sometimes, he was heard saying:

> "I would be satisfied if Allâh pardons me in the Hereafter."

He ordered all his governors all over the Islamic State to be kind even to animals for fear that he might be responsible for any injustice they might cause to people. He said:

> "I fear that if a mule stumbles in Iraq, I will be questioned as to why I did not pave the way for it."

Tears drew two black lines on his cheeks for fear that he might be punished by Allâh. Although he was told by the Prophet ﷺ that he would dwell in Paradise, he would pray most of the night in order to be acceptable to Allâh.

Sound Judgment

Some judgments given by 'Umar ؓ have become religious rules. One case was when he asked the Prophet ﷺ to order women to wear *Hijab* (Islamic dress). Allâh supported his opinion and Qur'ânic revelation came down ordaining the same. The Prophet ﷺ said:

> "If there were divinely inspired men in my nation, it would be 'Umar."

★★★

The End

As usual, 'Umar ﵁ made pilgrimage to Makkah in the beginning of the eleventh year of his rule. The Islamic state had by now spread over Syria, Egypt, Persia and some parts of the Byzantine Empire. This quick spread of Islam was hated and envied by all enemies of Islam. They would try now and then to thwart Islam but in vain.

'Umar ﵁ used to go to *Fajr* (Dawn) prayer unattended by any guards. He left his house to the mosque in the dark, ordered for the prayer to be performed and stood in front of the lines as leader of the prayer. A Persian named Fairuz had planned to kill the Caliph. He decided to do his crime during the prayer. As 'Umar ﵁ started the prayer, Fairuz stepped forward and stabbed him several times in his side with a dagger. He also killed other Muslims who were trying to get hold of him. 'Umar ﵁ retreated to the first row and ordered his son to complete the prayer as the leader. The persons behind him saw this criminal act by the Persian. They tried to catch him but he killed himself.

'Umar ﵁ was taken home. He asked who could be the man who stabbed him. They told him that it was Fairuz. 'Umar ﵁ thanked Allâh that the killer was not a Muslim. He was well aware that the enemies of Islam would not allow its message to be spread in peace.

Before dying, he selected six men and ordered that one among them to be selected as the Caliph. He also asked the permission of Aishah رضي الله عنها (the Prophet's wife) to be buried beside the Prophet ﷺ. She agreed although she wanted to keep the place for herself. Three days later 'Umar ﵁ passed away.

'Umar ﵁ was buried beside the Prophet ﷺ and Abu Bakr ﵁. He lied there in peace to meet with the Prophet ﷺ and his Companions on the Day of Judgment fully satisfied that he did his best to spread the Word of Allâh.

May Allâh bestow his mercy on 'Umar

رضي الله عنه, the best example of justice, for the great services he rendered to Islam and the Muslims.

We should all remember ‘Umar رضي الله عنه with great gratitude. Had it not been for the help of Allâh and the efforts exerted by ‘Umar رضي الله عنه, the Islamic State would not have spread over the world.